T0197370

Nighttime
FANTASY

Suzanne M. Shields

AuthorHouse™
1663 Liberty Drive
Bloomington, IN 47403
www.authorhouse.com
Phone: 1 (833) 262-8899

Because of the dynamic nature of the Internet, any web addresses or
links contained in this book may have changed since publication and
may no longer be valid. The views expressed in this work are solely those
of the author and do not necessarily reflect the views of the publisher,
and the publisher hereby disclaims any responsibility for them.

This book is printed on acid-free paper.

ISBN: 978-1-7283-7284-6 (sc)
ISBN: 978-1-7283-7285-3 (hc)
ISBN: 978-1-7283-7283-9 (e)

Library of Congress Control Number: 2020916899

Print information available on the last page.

Published by AuthorHouse 09/15/2020

author HOUSE®

"Nighttime Fantasy"

When I lay me down to sleep, monsters in my room do creep. Some are large and some are small, on the ceiling, on my wall. Never by day, always at night, they wander about and cause me such fright.

What do they want, and who could they be? This question nocturnally bothers me! I run out my door, and into mom's bed, and on her soft shoulder, I nestle my head.

She gives me a kiss, and a warm gentle hug. Says, "Nothing to fear, my little love bug." And as I lay next to my mommy so dear, I wonder why monsters don't visit in here.

"Nighttime Fantasy" Poem format as originally written.

When I lay me down to sleep,

Monsters in my room do creep.

Some are large and some are small,

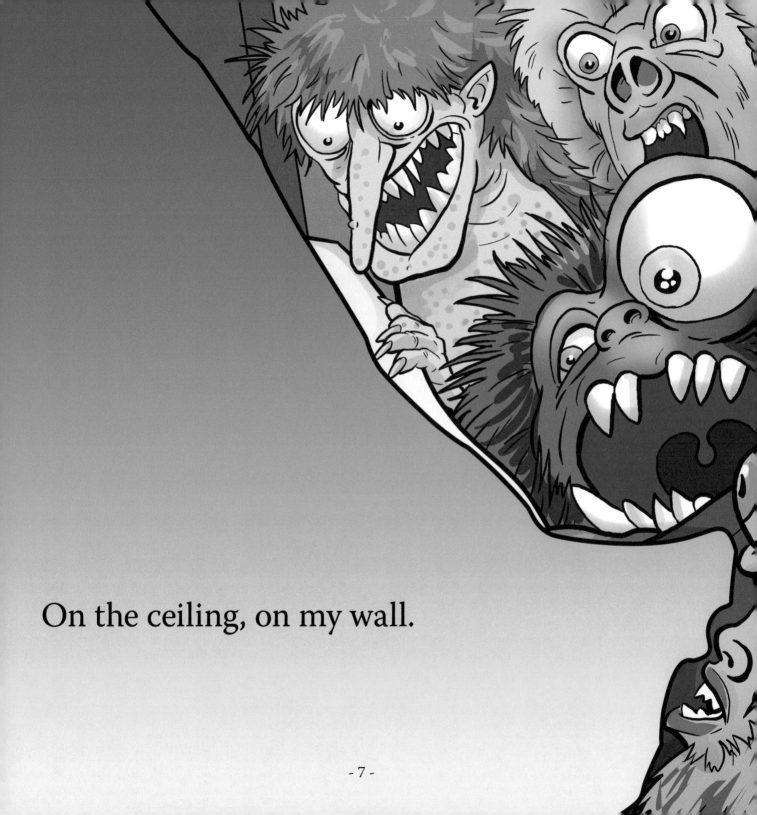

On the ceiling, on my wall.

Never by day, always at night,

They wander about and cause me such fright.

What do they want, and who could they be?

This question nocturnally bothers me!

I run out my door, and into mom's bed,

And on her soft shoulder, I nestle my head.

She gives me a kiss, and a warm gentle hug.

Says, "Nothing to fear, my little love bug."

And as I lay next to my mommy so dear,

I wonder why monsters don't visit in here.

Printed in the United States
by Baker & Taylor Publisher Services